HOCUS POCUS HOTEL

Hocus Pocus Hotel is published by Stone Arch Books
A Capstone Imprint
1710 Roe Crest Dr.
North Mankato, Minnesota 56003
www.capstonepub.com

Cataloging-in-Publication Data is available at the Library
of Congress website.

ISBN: 978-1-4342-6507-4 (library binding)

Summary: Abracadabra, the founder of the Hocus Pocus
Hotel has vanished! Charlie Hitchcock and Tyler Yu team
up again to solve this mystery and find their friend.

Photo credits: Shutterstock
Abracadabra Hotel Illustration: Brann Garvey
Designed by Kristi Carlson

Printed in China.
092013
007733LEOS14

The Wizard and the Wormhole

BY MICHAEL DAHL

ILLUSTRATED BY LISA K. WEBER

STONE ARCH BOOKS™
a capstone imprint

3 THE ABRACADABRA HOTEL

Table of

Contents

Impossible

From his desk near the back of Ms. Gimli's classroom, Charlie Hitchcock stared at the three impossible words.

ABRACADABRA IS MISSING.

Abracadabra, master of the impossible, the world's oldest living magician, missing? The same man who had made other people disappear, along with rabbits, airplanes, school buses, and the occasional elephant? How could he vanish?

If Abracadabra had disappeared on purpose, he would have let Charlie in on his plans. After all, the great performer — known as Brack to his friends — certainly thought of Charlie as a pal.

No way. Brack would have told me! Charlie thought. He scrunched the note up. *Or he would have told Ty, and Ty would have told me.*

Tyler Yu lived and worked at the world-famous Abracadabra Hotel. And while Charlie didn't exactly consider Ty his friend, the two boys had often worked together to solve puzzles surrounding the hotel's mysterious guests. It was Ty who had secretly handed the note to Charlie out in the hall, between classes. Charlie knew better than to say or ask anything at the time. Ty couldn't afford to let anyone know that he was on speaking terms with Charlie Hitchcock, the smartest kid in Blackstone Middle School, and therefore the school's biggest nerd.

If Brack didn't say anything to me or Ty, thought Charlie, *then his disappearance wasn't planned. An accident?*

Charlie heard an odd *tap-tap* sound.

"What's that tapping?" asked Ms. Gimli from the front of the classroom.

Scotter Larson raised his hand. "I believe," he began without being called on, "it's Morse Code, Ms. Gimli."

"Morse Code?" Ms. Gimli repeated. "Well, whoever is doing it should stop."

"It's not me, Ms. Gimli," said Scotter. The blond boy sat up straighter in his desk. "Even though I was the youngest Scout in the tri-state area to receive a badge for Morse Code."

Something hit Charlie on the shoulder. He looked up and saw Tyler Yu standing just outside the door of Ms. Gimli's room.

The tall boy looked angry. He always looked angry. He tapped harder against the doorframe with a pen.

"Impossible," said Scotter Larson. "It doesn't make sense."

Ms. Gimli turned from the whiteboard and looked at Scotter. "What is impossible?"

"The Morse Code message," Scotter said. "The Morse message says H-V-R-R-Y-V-P. But that's not a word."

Charlie wrote down the letters in his notebook.

H.V.R.R.Y.V.P.

Scotter may think it's not a word, he thought, *but it is. Two words, actually.*

Charlie knew that in order to solve a puzzle you sometimes needed to take into account unpredictable factors. And the most unpredictable factors were personalities.

In this case, the personality of the person actually sending the Morse code message: Tyler Wu. Ty knew a lot about secrets and strategy, but he wasn't the best speller.

Tyler's making a mistake, thought Charlie. *He's using three dots instead of two to spell a Morse letter. He doesn't mean V, he means U. He's telling me to hurry up!*

Charlie looked at Tyler. The tall boy's face was turning red. His eyes were glowing.

Charlie rushed up to Ms. Gimli. "Uh, may I go to the lavatory?" he whispered.

"Can't you wait until lunch?"

"I don't think so."

"Then hurry up," said the teacher.

"Hurry up?" said Scotter to himself.

He's figuring it out, thought Charlie. He gathered his things and left the room.

"What took you so long?" Ty spat out. "You saw the note!" He turned and headed down the hall. "And before you say anything, yeah, I know the Morse Code was spelled wrong. I did that on purpose so no one else would figure it out."

"Wait!" said Charlie, running alongside. "Where are you going?"

Tyler stopped. He fixed Charlie with a steely look, as if he were pinning the boy to the wall. "I thought you figured that out, too. Aren't you the smartest kid in school?"

Charlie said, "You're going to the hotel? Now? In the middle of the day?"

Tyler smiled, but it was a cold smile. "Wrong, Brainiac. *We're* going to the hotel. Now. In the middle of the day. Our friend needs us."

And that was all Charlie needed to hear.

Double Emergency

It was raining by the time Charlie and Ty reached the Abracadabra Hotel in an old section of downtown Blackstone.

The ancient building — known to its residents as the Hocus Pocus Hotel, but officially named for its founder, Abracadabra — raised its towers toward the dark, churning clouds.

When the boys walked through the glass double doors, they passed from rain, gloom, and thunder to bright lights, laughter, and excited voices. The vast lobby was stuffed with people.

"What's going on?" asked Charlie. "Is it a party?"

"Tyler!" yelled a voice. The boys saw a young girl elbowing her way through the crowd. It was Annie Solo, who worked at the front desk.

"Tyler," she said. "I'm so glad to see you. You got my text!"

"Text?" Ty said, frowning. "I don't have a phone. You must have had the wrong number."

"I beeped you, too," Annie said.

"Annie, you know I can't have my beeper on at school," Tyler said.

Charlie guessed that Tyler had probably been ignoring the girl's messages. Annie made it no secret that she had a crush on Tyler.

Ty, however, felt differently. He grabbed Charlie by the collar and started using him as a human plow to push through the crowd.

"Sorry, but I'm in the middle of an emergency here," said Ty.

"I'll say," said Annie, following closely. "This afternoon's the Friday special preview. And the tech guy never showed up for it, and I knew that you've worked the light booth before, so —"

"What are you talking about, Annie?" asked Charlie. It was hard for him to hear her while being shoved between men wearing suits and women in long gowns that glittered like plastic wrap.

"The magic show preview," she said. "The preview of David Dragonstone before tonight's big show! He goes on in half an hour, but we don't have anyone to run the lights for the stage."

"Annie," said Tyler, without stopping or looking back, "I can't right now."

"But you're not in school," Annie pointed out.

"Neither are you," Tyler shot back.

"I'm in a work program, remember?" said Annie. "Every Wednesday and Friday afternoon. What's your excuse?"

"Emergency," said Tyler. "Besides, you told me to come."

"Because your mother asked me to," Annie said. "And if she finds out you left school, but not to help me, then . . ."

Tyler's mother, Miranda Yu, was the hotel manager for the Abracadabra. His dad, Walter Yu, was the head chef of the hotel restaurant, the Top Hat. Although Charlie had met them only briefly, he knew they were deadly serious about work. He often wondered if any one of the Yus ever smiled.

Tyler stopped. The three of them had squeezed a path through the crowd and stood near the row of elevators. Ty's shoulders slumped, and he looked down at his boots.

"Okay, fine," he said. "I'll run the lights for the afternoon show. But I better get paid for it." He turned to Charlie. "You go up to Brack's place and search for clues. Find out where he went in the hotel."

"You said he was missing," said Charlie.

"Yeah, but he never left the hotel," Ty told him.

"How do you know that?" Charlie asked.

"Surveillance cameras," said Tyler.

"So that's what you were looking at in the office last night," said Annie.

Tyler ignored her. "There are cameras all over the lobby," he told Charlie. "See?" Charlie followed Ty's pointed finger and noticed small gold-colored gadgets attached to the lobby's pillars.

"We can see anyone going out or coming in through the hotel doors," said Ty. "There are more cameras at the loading dock in the alley. But Brack wasn't on any of them. He has to be somewhere in the building."

Unless he found a magic way out, thought Charlie.

"Brack was supposed to be at Dragonstone's rehearsal last night, but he never showed up," chimed in Annie.

"I know," said Ty. "That's why I'm worried. He's been gone eighteen hours now."

Charlie knew Brack would never miss a rehearsal. He was too good a performer for that. Was he hurt? Or sick? Brack was older than the hotel bearing his name, and old people sometimes had health problems.

"He's gone. Vanished," said Ty.

"Can the cameras tell us where Brack went?" asked Charlie.

"They only look at the exits and entrances," said Ty.

Annie grabbed Tyler's arm. "We need to hurry," she said. "They're opening the doors in ten minutes."

"Go up to Brack's and look for clues," said Ty. "Then come back here and we'll search the hotel together."

"I'd love to!" said Annie.

Tyler opened his mouth to object, but Annie quickly led him away from the crowd and through another door.

"Don't worry," Charlie called out to Ty's vanishing back. "I'll be fine."

Charlie entered an elevator and pushed the gold button at the very top.

Don't worry? he asked himself. *Who am I kidding? I skipped school, Brack is missing, and I don't know what I'm supposed to look for.*

It was the perfect time to worry.

Clues on the Carpet

The spring shower had grown into
a raging thunderstorm. Wind and rain
whipped fiercely around the tall downtown
buildings as Charlie ran from the shelter
of the elevator toward Brack's home. The
magician's house was perched on the rooftop
of the old hotel. It was surrounded by empty
flower gardens and leafless trees that stuck
out of cement pots like upside-down claws
scratching the air.

When Charlie reached the front door and grasped the knob, he was cold and soaked with rain.

I'm so stupid, thought Charlie. *I should have asked Annie for a key to get into Brack's place. Now what am I going to do?*

Charlie shivered and tried the knob. The door was unlocked. Cautiously, he stepped inside. The hall light was on. "Brack!" he called.

As he stepped forward, rain puddled on the carpet around his shoes. Charlie dropped his backpack on the floor and yelled again. "Brack!"

There was no answer.

Charlie felt odd looking through his friend's house while he was gone. As if he were breaking the law. But he knew he had to do it. He had to search for clues.

Like the empty cup on the table in a small sitting room. That was the only other room in Brack's apartment where the lights were on. The room was full of magical props from hundreds of stage shows. The walls were covered with colorful, old-fashioned posters. But the empty cup seemed out of place to Charlie.

He picked it up and sniffed. Yuck! Coffee. He hated the taste and smell of coffee. Come to think of it, so did Brack. So why was it there? For a guest?

Why are the lights on? he wondered. *Annie said Brack never showed up at the magic show rehearsal last night. Brack must have been here, and then disappeared before morning.*

Charlie noticed a table nearby that held leather-bound books and more magic props. In the middle of the table were two items that snagged his attention.

A cardboard tube lay on a yellow notepad. The tube was empty. A name was stamped at one end: LAND REGISTRAR, BLACKSTONE COUNTY.

On the yellow pad were a few words, scrawled in pencil.

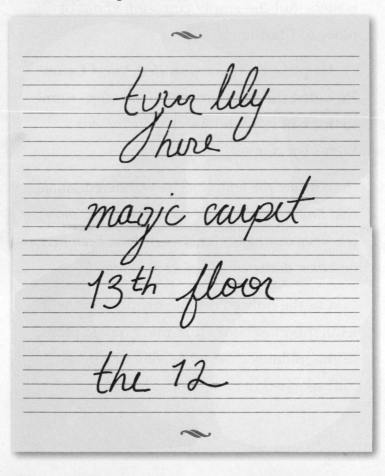

Tiger lily? Charlie stood back up and looked quickly around the room. There were no flowers in here. What did Brack mean?

And Charlie knew that the Hocus Pocus Hotel did not have a thirteenth floor. Not officially. It had a floor above the twelfth one, of course, but it wasn't numbered thirteen. It was called the fourteenth floor. Many hotels did the same trick. Lots of people were superstitious and refused to sleep on an unlucky thirteenth floor. So hotels just dropped the 13 and substituted 14 in its place.

Maybe Brack was writing about a magic trick for one of his shows.

Lightning flashed through the windows of the house.

I better get back downstairs, thought Charlie. He tore the paper off the pad and stuffed it into his backpack.

He made one last quick tour of the house to make sure the windows and other doors were locked. There was no way in or out, except through the front door. Charlie stood, his hand on the doorknob, looking out at the fierce storm.

Brack must have been in a hurry when he left, Charlie thought. *Otherwise he would have locked the door. Or maybe he realized he was hurrying to the rehearsal, and he just forgot.*

Charlie frowned.

Nothing in Brack's house seemed to be a real clue. The magician might have been visiting with an old friend who liked coffee. Maybe he'd been working on a new magic trick that involved carpets and flowers, and then ran down to the rehearsal. Nothing unusual.

Charlie picked up his backpack and froze.

On the damp carpet, lay an object he had not seen before. It had been hidden by his pack. He squatted down and picked it up. A clump of hair.

Fake red hair.

The Dragonstone Disappearance

"Find anything?" asked Ty when Charlie got back downstairs.

Charlie nodded. "Yeah," he said, reaching into his backpack. "Wait till you see —"

"Tyler!" yelled Annie. "It's about to start."

The three of them were standing inside the booth that controlled the lighting for the Abracadabra Theatre.

The booth was on the rear wall of the
theater, opposite the stage, and high above
the audience. Charlie could see the tops
of five hundred heads, facing the stage
and waiting for the entrance of David
Dragonstone.

"Here goes," said Ty, sliding a lever on
the huge control panel.

Bright lights lit up the stage and a
roar of applause shook the walls. David
Dragonstone — tall, thin, with piercing eyes
— walked out onto the stage and waved.

"That guy's the magician?" said Ty. "He
looks like a kid."

He has red hair, thought Charlie.

The boys and Annie watched the entire
show, which lasted an hour. Tyler kept busy
reading the light cues from sheets on a
clipboard.

Then came the final trick of the performance.

On the stage far below, bathed in brilliant light, several assistants strapped Dragonstone into a straitjacket. A chain was wrapped around his ankles. Then a hook was attached to the chain and the young, redheaded magician was hoisted into the air.

The audience gasped. Dragonstone rose higher and higher. He came to rest, thirty feet above the stage, upside down. Then, without warning, a strange man climbed onto the stage.

The stranger wore a flowing black robe. He had dark hair that hung to his shoulders and a black mustache and pointed beard. "Ladies and gentlemen," said the man in a commanding voice. "Behold, the amazing Dragonstone, in his final act of the evening."

He gestured to the young magician twisting high above him. "Dragonstone has amazed audiences throughout the world. It is my humble duty and great pleasure, as the Wizard DeVille, to announce this final feat of illusion and legerdemain."

"Leger what?" asked Ty.

"It means trickery," said Annie. "Like a trick that a magician can do with his hands."

Dragonstone can't use his hands, strapped in that jacket, thought Charlie. *There's no way out of it.*

"Behold!" cried the wizard. "And tremble with fear!"

The hook holding David Dragonstone snapped open. The magician plunged headfirst, still straitjacketed, toward the stage, thirty feet below.

The straitjacket hit the stage. But instead of a thud, it made hardly a sound.

The wizard, DeVille, ran over to the lifeless form. He lifted it up easily with one hand. It was only the straitjacket, and it was empty. Dragonstone had fallen toward the stage, but he never reached it. The redheaded magician had disappeared.

"Dragonstone has disappeared," shouted DeVille.

A member of the audience began clapping. Then another. And another. Soon everyone in the audience was cheering and shouting.

"What a trick!" said Annie.

"But who is that guy?" said Ty.

The magician named DeVille bugged Charlie, too. Something was not right. Now two magicians were missing.

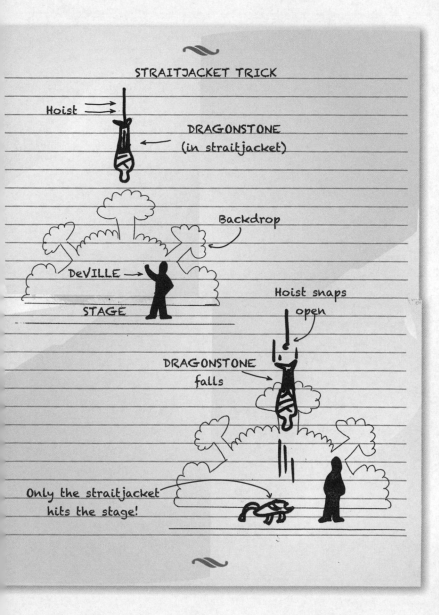

The Glass Keyhole

DeVille, his eyes flashing above his dark mustache, raised his gloved hands to the audience.

"Ladies and gentlemen," he said, "you have witnessed the power of Monsieur Dragonstone to disappear in midair. But where, I ask you, has he gone?"

The audience grew still. People who were standing sat back down.

"This is but the first half of the finale," said DeVille. "I now need a volunteer from the audience."

A young man stood up near the front of the stage.

"I know that guy," said Tyler, peering out the light booth window.

"That's Joey Bingham," said Charlie. "The news reporter. What's he up to?"

DeVille motioned for the reporter to join him onstage. "This young man shall be my witness," said DeVille. "And he will be your eyes." DeVille waved his hands again and a large screen was lowered onto the stage.

"Tyler!" yelled Annie. "The projector button."

"Oh yeah, right," said Ty. He quickly scanned the control panel and pressed a button. A flash of blue light hit the screen.

DeVille presented a small object to Joey Bingham. "Take this camera, young man," said the wizard. "And follow me." He turned to the audience. "Now, you shall see the amazing Dragonstone reappear in a completely different part of the hotel. Watch the screen."

Charlie and the others saw shapes and movement on the stage screen. They saw DeVille as he walked off the stage and through a door, into a hallway, and through the hotel lobby. DeVille stopped at the elevators and faced Joey's camera. "We shall now go up to the twelfth floor," said DeVille. "There, we will witness an even more incredible illusion."

Charlie turned to Ty, who was staring intently at the screen. "I'm going up there," Charlie said.

"Me too," said Tyler.

"But what about the booth?" said Annie.

"Nothing to it," said Ty. "Light on, lights off. Besides, the projector button will stay on through the rest of the trick."

"But what if —"

"I've got to make sure Hitchcock doesn't get into any trouble," said Ty. "He's too puny to take care of himself." The two boys rushed out of the light booth and reached the lobby elevators.

DeVille and Joey were already gone.

"Puny, huh?" asked Charlie.

"Get in the elevator," said Ty.

Ping! When the elevator doors slid open on the twelfth floor, the boys slipped out.

"Down there," said Tyler.

At the end of the hall, DeVille and Joey were turning a corner.

The boys rushed up to join them. Joey, hearing their footsteps, turned around, his camera facing them.

Great, thought Charlie. *Now the whole audience can see us.*

DeVille stopped when he saw the newcomers. He drew up his shoulders and addressed the camera, with great dignity, "Excellent. We have been joined by two new witnesses. Complete strangers, I assure you. They shall convince you, ladies and gentlemen of the audience, that what they see, what you see from your seats, is absolutely real!"

After a few more turns through the maze-like hallways, DeVille came to a sudden stop. "This is it," he said, and gestured to Joey. "Take a picture of that doorway."

"What the heck is that?" asked Joey.

"Have you seen that before?" Charlie whispered to Ty.

The taller boy nodded. "I avoid it when I come up here," he said. "There's no way to get through it."

The door was something that could only be seen in a hotel built by magicians. It was made of glass and led into another dim hallway that could be clearly seen on the other side. But no one could enter the hallway, because the door was more of a window than a door. It did not open. There were no hinges. In the exact center of the glass door was a small opening shaped like a keyhole.

DeVille's gleaming eyes shot at Tyler. "Since you work here, young man, then you must know that there is no way through this glass door."

Joey swung the camera up at the tall boy.

"Yeah, that's right," answered Ty. "It's just for fun. This is a trick door made by Abracadabra when he built the hotel. It's just sort of a joke."

"Or perhaps a challenge to other magicians," said DeVille. "And what is at the end of this hallway on the other side of the glass?"

"It connects to the other hallways," said Ty. "But you have to walk all the way around to reach it."

DeVille nodded. "Would you be so kind as to stand at the other end of that hallway?" he said. "You shall be our guard. Make sure no one gets in or out of the hallway."

Tyler looked at Charlie and shrugged. "Okay, fine," he said. Then he took off.

DeVille spoke to the camera.

"There is no one up here except myself and these three witnesses, ladies and gentlemen," he said. "I checked with the hotel staff, and no one is in any of the rooms on this floor. All the doors are locked. But —" He pulled a long, yellow ribbon from his coat. "Someone invisible is with us."

A ghost? thought Charlie.

"The spirit of Dragonstone," said DeVille, as if answering the boy's thought. "He is in that mysterious hallway. Unable to reach us through the solid glass door. But, by using this ribbon which I obtained from my brother wizards in Katmandu, I shall open a mystic wormhole and rescue the invisible Dragonstone."

DeVille rolled up a piece of the ribbon and then stuffed it through the tiny keyhole, where it cascaded in a long strand down the other side.

"I shall hold this end," said the magician, keeping a firm hold on the ribbon.

Next, DeVille rolled a metal frame in front of the glass door. The magician pulled down black curtains on the frame, effectively screening the glass door from the viewers' eyes. But the ribbon passed through the curtains. DeVille stood just outside the frame, where Joey's camera could still see him, one end of the ribbon still in his hand.

"Watch the ribbon," said DeVille. "I shall pull it back through the keyhole and onto this side of the solid glass door."

Slowly, ever so slowly, the dark haired magician pulled the yellow ribbon through the black curtains. It kept coming.

What's the big deal? thought Charlie. *He's just pulling the ribbon back through the keyhole. Why won't he let us watch it happen?*

"Hey!" shouted Joey.

The ribbon stopped. DeVille held it in both hands now, and Charlie could see that the ribbon wasn't coming any farther. It must have caught on something.

"How could it be stuck?" asked DeVille. "The keyhole is smooth, and there is nothing between it and the curtains. Perhaps it has found something in the wormhole."

Charlie felt a growing coldness along his spine. "Mr. Hitchcock," said DeVille. "Would you be so kind as to pull the curtains open for our audience?"

Charlie walked over, grabbed a curtain, and yanked it aside. Joey almost dropped his camera. In front of them, on the same side of the glass door as them and DeVille, stood the redheaded Dragonstone, with the yellow silk ribbon tied around his waist.

The Third Disappearance

David Dragonstone bowed to the camera. "Thank you, Monsieur DeVille," he said, smiling, "for rescuing me from the Beyond. And thank you, everyone, for coming to this afternoon's premiere."

DeVille reached over and snapped off the camera. "Magnificent," said DeVille, clapping the other magician on the back.

"What's going on?" came a voice.

Tyler ran up to the glass door from the other side. His eyes grew wide as he saw Dragonstone. "Hey, how did he get over there?"

"Through a wormhole," said Joey.

Charlie noticed a worried look on the redheaded man's face. But DeVille gave him a reassuring look. "Don't worry," said DeVille. "That young man in the elegant T-shirt and jeans is another volunteer. He was making sure no one could enter from the far end."

"Ah, thank you for your assistance," Dragonstone said to Tyler. Turning to DeVille, he added, "We should return to the stage."

"But how did you get here?" asked Joey. "You weren't inside that flimsy frame. You couldn't hide inside a curtain."

"There was no one in the hallway when I got to the other side," said Tyler.

"Wizardry," said DeVille with a wave of his hand.

The magicians walked off, followed by a chattering Joey, trying to get a scoop for his paper.

"I can see the headline now," said Joey. "The Hair-Raising Houdini of the Hocus Pocus Hotel!"

"Young man!" came the dwindling voice of the retreating wizard. "It's the Abracadabra, if you don't mind."

Tyler and Charlie stared at one another through the solid glass door.

"How'd he do it, Hitch?" asked Tyler. Both boys felt the smooth glass. It was solid. And the keyhole was clearly too small for anyone to pass through.

"You didn't see anything over there?" asked Charlie.

"Nothing," said Ty. "And that hall is long. I could barely see the black curtain come down over the door. But I did hear a funny noise."

"Funny?"

"Like a thump. Or someone jumping."

Tyler shook his head as if to clear it. "I'm just glad this stupid show is over. Meet me at the elevators and we'll head up to Brack's."

Charlie ran back to the elevators. On the way he glanced at the wallpaper in the hall. It was covered with prints of fancy-looking flowers. Tiger lilies? No, they looked more like roses.

The hall with the elevators was quiet. The two magicians and Joey must have already gone back to the theater.

As Charlie stood and waited for Ty, he thought back to the amazing illusion he had just witnessed. How did Dragonstone appear? Had he been hiding somewhere in that hallway? Even if he was, how did he pass through the solid glass door? Joey had been right; no one could have hidden in that frame or curtains. Dragonstone must have come from the other side of the glass. But how?

And what was taking Tyler so long?

"Ty," shouted Charlie. He felt as if he were standing inside Brack's empty house again.

No answer. Charlie listened but didn't hear any approaching footsteps. "Ty!" he called.

Charlie ran down several halls, hoping he was going in the direction of the blocked hallway.

He could just make out the curtains that had been left on the other side of the glass door. This was the place.

So where was Tyler? They should have run into each other.

Charlie called a few more times, but heard nothing. He started to sweat. Something was wrong.

Charlie ran back to the elevators. Still no Ty.

He waited a few more minutes. He shouted one last time. Then he pushed the button to call an elevator and descended to the main floor, alone.

Beard and Mustache

Charlie pushed through crowds of people streaming through the lobby as they exited the theater. They were heading toward the front doors, where they opened umbrellas to face the pouring rain, or waved their arms for honking taxicabs.

When Charlie reached the front desk he was disappointed to not see Tyler. He was surprised to see Annie, though. Her familiar smile was twisted into a frown.

"Where have you been?" she said. "Where's Tyler?"

"I don't know," said Charlie. "I thought he was down here."

"Well, he's not!" she said. "And I had to figure out those lights all by myself. The audience was in the dark for ten minutes!"

"He told me to meet him at the elevators, but he never showed up," said Charlie.

Wait a minute. Tyler said something else before I left him, thought Charlie. *Something that didn't make sense at the time.*

"Typical," said Annie, folding her arms. She looked back at the front desk, where another young woman with thick dark hair was frantically helping five customers at the same time. "I have to get to work," she said.

"Wait," said Charlie. "I think Tyler disappeared."

"Of course he did," said Annie, walking away.

"I mean — disappeared!"

Annie stopped in midstride. She turned to look at Charlie. "You mean like Brack?"

"I'm worried," said Charlie. "After everything happened, Ty and I were supposed to meet back at the elevators. Like I said, he never showed up. Then I ran around all the halls but didn't see him."

"I hope he's not hurt," Annie said.

"Was DeVille right?" asked Charlie. "There's no one on that floor?"

Annie nodded. "And all the doors are locked." She shook her head. "Poor, poor Tyler."

"Annie!" The girl at the desk looked upset.

"I'll be right there, Cozette," called
Annie.

"But we need to find Ty," said Charlie.
"And Brack."

Annie stepped toward Charlie and
grabbed his hand. Suddenly, she looked very
serious. Annie spoke in a low tone. Her lips
moved close to his ear. She whispered, "Meet
me on the twelfth floor in ten minutes. We'll
look for them together." Then she stood up
and hurried back to the desk.

As she walked away, Charlie noticed that
he was holding something in his hand. *She
was just giving me a key.* It was a passkey to
all the rooms in the hotel.

Instead of going to the twelfth floor,
Charlie headed backstage. He remembered
the hunk of red hair from Brack's carpet. He
was sure it had something to do with the
redheaded David Dragonstone.

In the theater, men and women were moving props, sweeping the stage, and guiding racks of costumes through the workspace. All the lights were on.

"Excuse me," said Charlie to a woman walking past with a case full of snakes. "Can you tell me where the magicians are?"

The woman used the case to point. "The dressing room's over that way," she said.

"Thanks," Charlie said. "Hey, are those snakes real?"

"Maybe," the woman said, smiling.

Charlie rushed over to the dressing room. It was locked. He put his ear to the door and heard nothing inside.

Making sure no one was watching him, he used the passkey and let himself in. Then he groped for a light switch near the door.

When the lights came on, Charlie found himself in a long narrow room with a row of mirrors along one wall. In front of the mirrors ran a low counter and several chairs. Plastic containers sat on the counter. Opening them, Charlie saw pencils, brushes, sponges, and tubes of different colors of makeup.

Turbans and top hats hung from hooks on the walls, along with capes, several straitjackets, and an undersea diver's outfit. Closets stood at each end of the room. Charlie searched through those as well. He wasn't exactly sure what he was looking for, but he knew he had to start somewhere. *I found the red hair when I wasn't expecting it,* he thought, *so if I just keep looking, maybe —*

Then he saw it, hanging on a hook at the back of one of the closets. A fake beard and mustache, both made of red hair. A section of hair on one side of the beard was missing.

Charlie pulled the red hair from his pocket and held it up to the beard.

A perfect match.

So Dragonstone had been upstairs talking to Brack. But how did the hair end up on the floor? Did Brack pull it off the man's face? Was there a struggle?

Charlie grew more worried about the missing magician. And Ty.

I've got to find them, he thought.

Charlie stuffed the beard into his backpack. He was backing out of the closet, when he heard a noise. Someone was unlocking the door.

He pushed through the costumes toward the back of the closet. He flattened against the wall and slid behind a dark furry robe that looked like a bearskin. Something scraped at his side, and he almost gasped.

In the dim light that filtered into the closet from the dressing room, he saw what had made the scraping sound. A rolled-up piece of blue paper leaned against the wall. On the upper edge he saw an official looking stamp. LAND REGISTRAR, BLACKSTONE COUNTY

Like the one in Brack's house, thought Charlie. It was too much of a coincidence that the young magician's closet held two items from the home of the missing Abracadabra. As quietly and quickly as he could, Charlie slipped the paper roll inside his backpack.

The door to the dressing room was opening. Charlie heard footsteps. A small thud. Someone breathing. Then everything went black. The lights had snapped off. Slowly, the door squeaked shut, and he heard the lock click.

Charlie hated the dark. It was the one thing that truly frightened him. He wasn't bothered by heights, spiders, snakes, or even tight spaces. In the light, at least, you could see those things. But in the dark, you were never sure what was there.

Was someone still in the room with him?

Charlie held his breath. Then he counted to a hundred. When he still heard nothing from the dressing room, he silently shuffled out of the closet. Moving through the hanging clothes in the darkness felt like walking through a crowd of people. Or through thick black curtains.

Black curtains! That's what Ty had said upstairs. Something about DeVille's curtains that didn't sound right.

Charlie slid his hands gently along the wall. He felt the doorframe and then the knob.

He turned the knob, and then pulled the door open. The lights from the stage were almost blinding.

Then he saw, on the counter by the mirror, a huge vase that hadn't been there before. It held a dozen roses and a small card. He reached over and read the card.

CONGRATULATIONS
ON YOUR PREVIEW!
MAGNIFIQUE!
Th____DeV.

Charlie sighed, relieved. The unseen footsteps hadn't been looking for him. They had simply dropped off the flowers. But what an odd way to sign your name. "The DeV.?"

Charlie replaced the card, closed the door, and hurried back to the elevators to show Annie what he had found.

The Stairs Between

"When was Brack supposed to meet Dragonstone last night?" asked Charlie.

"The rehearsal was at eight o'clock," answered Annie. "When Brack never showed up, we called upstairs, but he didn't answer."

They were standing in a hallway on the twelfth floor. They figured that floor was the best place to start their search for Ty. And if they found Ty, they might find Brack.

Charlie figured it was too much of a coincidence that both friends had vanished within 24 hours of each other. Their disappearances had to be connected.

"And Dragonstone was there already?" asked Charlie.

Annie nodded. "He got to the hotel right before the rehearsal. He didn't even have time to eat or go to his room. And while we waited onstage, he said that he wanted Brack to introduce his final act, the Empty Straitjacket."

"Really?" said Charlie. "So who was that DeVille guy?"

"A friend of Mr. Dragonstone's," said Annie. "When the rehearsal was almost over and Brack still hadn't shown up, Dragonstone called DeVille. DeVille came to the hotel this morning."

"This morning?"

"Yes, right after Tyler left for school."

"So when did they have time to rehearse the Glass Door Trick?" asked Charlie.

"I'm not sure about that," said Annie. "I don't think Dragonstone even mentioned it last night. It seemed like something DeVille came up with on his own."

There's something fishy about that, thought Charlie. But if Brack disappeared last night, Dragonstone might not be involved. Not if he was at rehearsal the whole time Brack was absent. Still, magicians were awfully tricky characters.

"Now what was it you wanted to show me?" asked Annie, sidling up closer to him.

Charlie pulled out the fake red beard and mustache from his backpack and explained them to her.

Then he knelt down on the thick hallway carpet and unrolled the blue paper he had found in the dressing room closet. Annie knelt down next to him.

"I found this in Dragonstone's dressing room," Charlie told her. "I'm sure it came out of an empty tube I found up at Brack's place. This stamp is on both of them." He pointed to the official words at the edge of the paper. He saw two more words he hadn't noticed before in the dim closet: ORIGINAL COPY.

Annie gasped. "It's the hotel," she said. "The Hocus Pocus — I mean, the Abracadabra. It's the whole hotel."

The blue roll of paper was actually made up of several sheets. And as Charlie stared at the top sheet in front of them, he realized Annie was right. These were blueprints for the old hotel.

It made sense that Brack would have kept them over the years, knowing how much the building meant to him.

"There's the theater," Annie said, pointing. "There's the lobby. Those circles are the pillars. There are the elevators."

Charlie flipped through the sheets. One of them showed a plan of the roof. "That's Brack's place," he said.

"See if you can find the twelfth floor," said Annie. "See if it has the glass door and keyhole in it."

"Good idea," said Charlie. He separated all the sheets and laid them out next to each other. Soon the hallway seemed to be re-carpeted with blue paper.

"There must be a dozen pages," said Annie.

"One for each floor," said Charlie.

But though they carefully examined each sheet, they could not find one for Floor 12.

"Here's fourteen," said Annie. "Twelve is missing!"

"No," said Charlie. "It's been stolen. The twelfth floor is where the magic act took place and the floor where Ty disappeared. Someone took that page on purpose."

"Mr. Dragonstone?" whispered Annie.

"Look at this," said Charlie. He pulled a page from the far end of the sheets.

"It's the whole hotel," said Annie.

Charlie liked the drawing. Faint white lines against a blue background showed the entire building, floor by floor, room by room.

"Here's the glass door," Annie said. "See?"

"Aha!" he said. "That's how it was done!"

A thump sounded somewhere in the hall.

"What was that?" whispered Annie.

"Footsteps?" asked Charlie.

They both held their breath and listened. The thumping stopped.

"The only way to get to these floors is by elevator, right?" whispered Charlie.

"And the stairwells," said Annie. "Every hotel needs stairs in case there's a fire. Then the elevators shut off, and even if you're on the twentieth floor, you have to use the stairs."

"Where are they?" said Charlie.

After a few moments of scanning the sheets, they found the drawing of the stairwell on the west side of the building. Something looked odd.

"Why is that flight of stairs longer than the others?" Charlie asked.

Annie peered closer. "You're right. The stairs from twelve to fourteen are longer. Weird."

A light exploded in Charlie's brain. *That's it, that's it!* he thought.

"Are you going to be sick?" asked Annie.

"The stairs!" he shouted. "The stairs!"

They heard another thump. This one seemed closer.

Charlie jumped to his feet. "We don't have any time to lose. Come on, where's the door to the stairs?"

Annie's face was pale. "But Charlie, those noises . . ."

"If I'm right," said Charlie, "I think someone is trying to communicate with us."

"A ghost?" asked Annie.

"No," said Charlie with a smile. "Ty."

Taking Steps

Annie led Charlie down three hallways,
up a short flight of steps, along another hall
curved like a macaroni noodle, and at last
to a metal door decorated with brass rabbits.
The heavy door opened swithout a creak.
Inside the echoing stairwell, the bannisters
gleamed with dark wood. Charlie wished
it were brighter in the stairwell. The small
lamps shaped like tulips provided very little
light.

"Up to the fourteenth floor," he said. "And count the steps."

They climbed to the next landing, turned, and climbed a second flight of stairs to reach a metal door with a brass "XIV" stamped at the top. "How many steps?" asked Charlie.

"Seventeen on each flight," said Annie. "So thirty-four steps between the twelfth floor and the fourteenth."

"Great," said Charlie. "Now we go up to the fifteenth."

Once they reached the fifteenth floor's landing, Annie looked amazed. "Only nine steps for each flight."

"That's eighteen in all," said Charlie. "So the space between twelve and fourteen is twice the height between the other floors."

Annie gasped. "Which means . . ."

Charlie smiled. "There's a thirteenth floor!"

Annie ran back down to the fourteenth floor, and then half a flight below that. Charlie followed her.

Annie searched the wall beneath the dim tulips. "I don't see any way in," she said.

"I don't think there's a door here," said Charlie. "I think the entrance is on the twelfth or fourteenth floor. My guess is that Dragonstone and DeVille have rooms on fourteen."

"Right," said Annie. "Two rooms next to each other."

"Let's go back to the hall on the twelfth floor. Where they did the magic trick," said Charlie. "I know how Dragonstone disappeared on stage, but it's —"

Annie stopped him. "You do?" she said.

"Simple mirrors," said Charlie. "And some legerdemain. But I'm still puzzled about the keyhole trick. How did Dragonstone appear behind that glass door in the first place? I think it has something to do with the thirteenth floor." He was also sure that the mysterious, hidden floor had something to do with the disappearance of his two friends.

Annie and Charlie passed through the metal door carved with rabbits and ran along the curving hallway. Wind rattled the hall's windows. Lightning flashed. The storm was growing stronger.

Beep . . . beep . . .

Annie stopped and fished something out of her pocket. "No, it's my beeper. So Mrs. Yu can reach us wherever we are in the hotel. It's a big place, you know." Annie groaned. "It's a 999. That means an emergency."

Minutes later, the two were walking through the hotel lobby again. It seemed empty to Charlie, now that the crowds from the preview magic show were gone.

But when he and Annie walked around one of the tall marble pillars, Charlie stopped in his tracks. A familiar figure stood at the front desk, his face cruel and triumphant, his arms folded across his chest as he spoke to Mr. and Mrs. Yu, Tyler's parents. "I shall be taking steps —" the figure was saying.

"Mr. Theopolis!" said Charlie.

The magician turned a sour face toward the boy. "Please, young man. The Great and Powerful Theopolis," he said. "And soon to be greater and more powerful."

Miranda Yu, in a sleek purple suit, looked unhappy. "I find this highly irregular, Mr. Theopolis," she said.

"It's completely regular, I assure you," Theopolis said. "And also legal."

Walter Yu took off his chef's hat and twisted it in his hands. Miranda Yu's face grew red. "You can't be serious," she said.

"Deadly serious," said Theopolis. "Which is why I checked everything with the Registrar's office before I came here."

Registrar! thought Charlie.

"If Brack does not make his special payment for the hotel's mortgage within the next twenty-four hours," said Theopolis with a toothy grin, "then the Abracadabra Hotel is mine!"

Deadline for Abracadabra

"What's going on?" cried Annie.

Mrs. Yu sighed. "It's not your problem, Annie," she said. "Don't worry about it."

Theopolis smiled widely. "In fact, it's everyone's problem. If that fraud Brack doesn't come up with the payment, then you, young lady, are out of a job."

Annie opened her mouth, but nothing came out except a tiny squeak.

The magician picked a piece of lint off his sleeve with one of his snow-white gloves. Charlie thought he looked dressed for a performance, with his perfect suit and long swirling cape.

"Is he right?" asked Annie. "Can he take away the hotel?"

Miranda Yu held her hand to her forehead as if she had a headache. "This is impossible," she said.

Walter Yu looked at Annie. "I'm afraid he may be right," he said. "Brack always makes payments at a certain time every month. It's part of the contract. And if he doesn't make a payment by tomorrow —"

"If he doesn't make the payment by tomorrow," interrupted Miranda Yu, "then the hotel is forfeit. In other words, the hotel would automatically change ownership."

"To me," finished the smug Theopolis. "It all dates back to the very beginning of the hotel, when Abracadbra and I were dear friends."

"That's hard to believe," Charlie muttered.

"Friendship is a tricky thing," said Theopolis. "Especially between magicians. Especially when one magician steals a trick from another and . . ." He stopped. His ears were the color of ripe tomatoes. The magician cleared his throat, smoothed out his cape, and resumed his speech.

"Abracadabra and I were partners. He had the vision for this hotel. I had the cash. At the time, I was the world's most sought-after performer. I was planning a tour and had no interest in overseeing the actual building. So I gave Brack the money, and he said he would repay me. Then I went on my tour and left this dreadful country behind."

"Brack did repay you," said Mrs. Yu. "He repays you every month, on time."

"Yes, dear lady," said Theopolis. "But as you know, our agreement includes an interesting clause in the contract. If Brack fails to make payments on this pile of bricks, then the ownership defaults to me."

"That's crazy," said Charlie. "Can't someone else make the payments for him? Like Mrs. Yu?"

"No," said the sneering magician. "The contract says that Abracadabra must pay. It must be his signature on the check. Or his skinny little fingers that hand over the cash. And, as an old friend, I would certainly give him a few days to make his payment, but . . . well, he doesn't seem to be around, does he?"

Theopolis's smile disappeared. "I shall be back tomorrow at this same time," he said.

"And if Brack is still not here," he went on, "then I shall expect your resignations within the week." He glanced around the lobby. "This used to be such a lovely place in its day. Ah, well, a renovation is clearly in order. And a more competent staff. Good day." With a swirl of his cape, he vanished into the shadows of the vast lobby.

Mr. Yu patted his wife's shoulder. "Don't worry, dear. We'll think of something."

Mrs. Yu glanced over at her husband. "I'm worried about Tyler. I've been beeping him for the past half hour."

Annie grabbed Charlie's hand and pulled him behind a pillar. "We have to find Brack right now!" she said. "And Tyler."

If not, Annie and Tyler and his parents would have to find new jobs, maybe a new home.

A crowd of people, carrying umbrellas and shaking the rain from their coats, entered the lobby from outside. A few photographers were flashing cameras and shoving microphones into wet, smiling faces.

Annie groaned. "I forgot all about the magic show."

"Another one?" Charlie asked.

"The real one. It starts in a couple hours, but people come early to get good seats."

Charlie recognized grabbed Annie's hand. "Let's head up to the fourteenth floor. We haven't been there yet, and that's where the two magicians are staying."

Riding in the elevator, Annie complained about Theopolis. "He's such a snake!" she said. "The way he looks at people. Ew! And even his clothes. He dresses up like a big shot, like he's better than us."

Charlie's thoughts were elsewhere. Why did Theopolis want the hotel now? Did he need money? Was he no longer in demand as the world's most sought-after performer?

"You're right, he did look awfully dressed up," said Charlie. "He even wore those white magician gloves." That made him think. "Did you notice anything else about his clothes?"

"Just that he looked like he was going onstage," said Annie, sourly.

"They were perfect," said Charlie.

"His clothes?"

"Perfectly dry."

Annie's eyes lit up slowly. "And there's a thunderstorm outside."

"A big thunderstorm," added Charlie. "There should have been some rain on his clothes. Or his shoes."

"And he didn't have an umbrella," Annie said. "He came from inside the hotel."

When Charlie thought about it, this whole mystery was all about where people were and when.

He listed everything in his notebook.

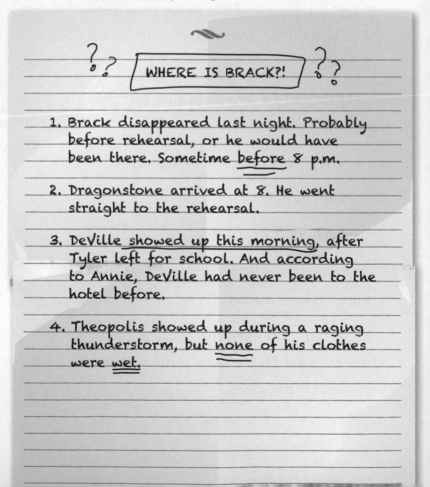

??? WHERE IS BRACK?! ???

1. Brack disappeared last night. Probably before rehearsal, or he would have been there. Sometime before 8 p.m.

2. Dragonstone arrived at 8. He went straight to the rehearsal.

3. DeVille showed up this morning, after Tyler left for school. And according to Annie, DeVille had never been to the hotel before.

4. Theopolis showed up during a raging thunderstorm, but none of his clothes were wet.

When the elevator let them out on the fourteenth floor, Annie led Charlie toward the magicians' rooms.

"Did you really mean it when you said you knew how the trick was done?" asked Annie. "The wormhole trick?"

"Sure," Charlie said. "I saw it on the blueprint. That glass door doesn't open. It has no hinges. But you can get around it."

"How?" Annie asked.

"It slides," said Charlie. "The glass can slide into the wall on either side, several inches at least. You noticed how skinny Dragonstone was, right? He slid the door to one side and squeezed around it. Then he slid it back in place, grabbed the end of the ribbon, and tied it around his waist."

"Wow," said Annie. "It seems so easy when you explain it. Not like magic at all."

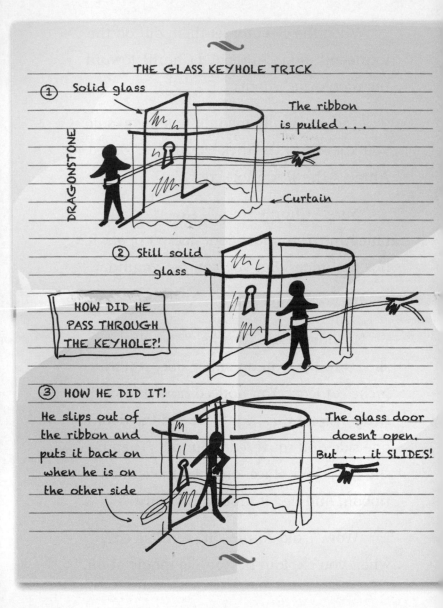

"I know," said Charlie. "Most tricks are like that once you know how they're done. Here, let me show you on the blueprint."

He reached into his backpack to gather the rolls. That's when he saw the folded piece of paper.

"What's that?" asked Annie.

"I forgot to show you," said Charlie, unfolding the yellow paper. "I found this upstairs with Brack's stuff, too. I figured it was important. Magic carpets and stuff, see?"

Annie looked at it carefully. "What does 'turn lily' mean?" she asked.

"That says 'Tiger lily here,'" said Charlie.

"No, it doesn't. It says 'Turn lily there.' Lilies. Like these on the wall." Annie pointed to the flowery wallpaper.

Flowers with a Twist

Charlie Hitchcock stared at the three words. It actually read TURN LILY THERE. Of course! Once you knew how to read it, the letters looked different, made another kind of sense. Charlie forgot that in order to solve a puzzle he needed to take into account unpredictable factors. And the most unpredictable factors were people. Their likes and dislikes, their voice, their walk, their clothes, and even their handwriting.

tiger lily
Shore

"Annie, you're a genius!" said Charlie.

"I am?" she said, smiling. "Thanks."

"These lilies," Charlie said, pointing to the wallpaper. "They're not the same as the flowers down on the twelfth floor."

"No," said Annie. "Each floor has a different flower. Roses, lilies, tulips, violets. I think that was Mr. Brack's idea, because he likes flowers."

"This writing is important," said Charlie, waving the yellow paper in his fist. "And it has something to do with the thirteenth floor, which is just below our feet. And something to do with a magic carpet. And whoever was visiting Brack last night saw his notes. These notes."

"So now what?" asked Annie.

"'Turn lily there,'" Charlie said. "I wonder where 'there' is? Well, we might as well head to the magicians' rooms. But let's keep an eye on the wallpaper. Maybe there's a hidden code or something."

As Annie led them toward the magicians' rooms, Charlie kept his eyes trained on the lilies that flowed past them on the wallpaper. He started feeling dizzy from staring at the repeating pattern of flowers.

"Here we are," said Annie. She had stopped between two doors. On the floor next to the wall lay several trays of half-eaten food, empty glasses, and a single coffee cup.

Charlie stuffed the yellow paper in his pocket. He felt something else.

The red hair.

The hair that matched the fake beard. If the hair was fake, then whoever was visiting Brack was in disguise. And no one would wear a disguise except someone who might be recognized.

"Theopolis!" said Charlie.

"Where?" said Annie, turning around.

"Upstairs, last night," said Charlie. "That's who visited Brack. He was the one who took the blueprints so he could get information about the hotel. And he's stayed inside the hotel ever since."

"But I thought Mr. Dragonstone and DeVille used the blueprints to figure out that trick with the glass door," said Annie.

"Yeah, you're right," said Charlie.

"So how did the blueprints get from Mr. Theopolis to the dressing room for Mr. Dragonstone?" she asked.

That's the big question, thought Charlie. *How* did *the blueprints get in there?*

"Charlie," Annie said slowly. "Look." She was pointing at the carpet.

There was a pattern in the carpet. A rectangle made of twisting lines of gold and turquoise and emerald and cream.

"It's beautiful," said Annie. "Like something out of the *Arabian Nights.*"

"Yeah, like something from *Aladdin,*" said Charlie. "It looks like —"

"A magic carpet," they said together.

DeVille's Trick

Charlie took a deep breath. "Remember what Brack wrote down."

"'Turn lily there,'" said Annie. They both turned to the wallpaper on either side of the hall and examined the painted flowers.

One of the lilies in the wall was not painted. It was actually a small plaster flower on the wallpaper itself, blending in with the two-dimensional flowers around it.

"I found it! I found it!" Annie said.

One of the magicians' doors opened abruptly. "Who is making all that noise?" A man stuck out his head and looked at Annie and Charlie. His expression was not kind.

His face made Charlie think of a million things all at once. He thought of the fake red beard. Someone in disguise having coffee with Brack last night. Someone reading Brack's writing as the old magician had been studying his precious blueprint. He thought of the signature on the card in Dragonstone's room. The writer had not written "The DeV." The writer had made a mistake. He had started writing the wrong word and then changed his mind.

Then Charlie thought of the Glass Door trick. How the French wizard DeVille had told Ty to stand at the far end of the hall since he knew his way around there.

And how the man had shouted at Charlie, calling him "Hitchcock," and ordering him to pull aside the black curtains to reveal Dragonstone.

How did DeVille know that Ty worked at the hotel? They never saw each other. Ty had already left for school before the Frenchman arrived. And how did he know Charlie's last name?

How did DeVille know? Because he had been to the hotel before. In fact, that's how the blueprint got from Theopolis to the dressing room. The same man who stole the papers also hid them. The same man who saw the blueprint last night, saw it during the rehearsal, and then suggested the Glass Door and Wormhole finale to Dragonstone's Empty Straitjacket trick after the rehearsal. Because he was the only person who knew the secret of the glass door besides Brack.

One person. A single person behind two beards, one red and one black.

"Theopolis!" cried Charlie.

"You meddling little brat!" said the magician, stepping into the hall. "You're always ruining my plans!"

"When Dragonstone called you, his friend 'DeVille,' to substitute for Brack, you were already inside the hotel," said Charlie.

"I'll make sure you never leave this hotel again," said Theopolis. "I'll deal with you like I dealt with Brack!"

"You're angry with him just because he revealed one of your tricks?" said Charlie. He was stalling for time.

"Just? Just?!" The magician's face contorted with rage. "A magician's tricks are his life. I was never able to use that trick again."

"You've never stolen a trick?" asked Annie.

Theopolis laughed. "I may have borrowed one or two. But I transform them. In my hands they become true miracles."

Charlie and Annie heard a sound behind them in the hall. "This is great," came a voice. "Just what I need for my scoop." Joey Bingham stepped out of the shadows. He held a video camera aimed at the arguing trio.

"Young man," said Theopolis. "Have you been recording all this time?"

"Mostly," said Joey with a big grin. "Keep talking. This is great stuff."

"What're you doing here?" Charlie asked.

"I've been here all day," said Joey. "I kept seeing you two running around and always going back to the elevator. I knew something was up." He laughed. "Up? Get it?"

Theopolis completely changed his manner. He became smooth and friendly. He sleeked his hair and bowed toward the camera. "Would you like a quick interview before the big show?" he said. "Learn how a famous performer prepares for the stage?"

"No," said Charlie. "You want something better than that, Joey. Something more exclusive. Something amazing. Something like how a magic trick is performed."

"No!" said Theopolis.

"Yeah," said Joey.

"Like the secret of the falling magician," Charlie said. "How did Dragonstone disappear from his straitjacket and then end up on the twelfth floor?"

Theopolis took a step toward the boys. "You're just like that thief Brack!" he said, snarling.

Charlie faced Joey's camera and spoke as quickly as could. "The secret is simple. There's a second straitjacket stuck to the back of the real one Dragonstone wears. He probably has a string or flap he can secretly pull with his hand. When he falls, the second jacket pops off and falls toward the stage. Dragonstone, still inside the first one, falls behind a trick mirror onstage. They both hit the ground at the same time."

"It looked like a cool trick," said Annie.

"It was," said Charlie. "And is. Dragonstone needs to be very skilled at timing, and at falling. He probably lands on some kind of safety net behind the trick mirrors. But it takes a lot of skill to fall and not break your neck."

Annie smiled. "And didn't you tell me earlier how Dragonstone passed through that solid glass door, too?"

"Enough, enough!" cried the magician. He folded his arms and looked down at Charlie. "What do you want?" he asked.

"I don't want anything," said Charlie. "But I'm sure Brack would like to keep his hotel."

"The hotel is mine," shouted the magician. "And so is that video camera!"

Another door popped open. A tall, red-headed man appeared. He stepped into the hall pulling on a pair of gloves.

"What's all this noise?" asked David Dragonstone. "Monsieur DeVille! You aren't dressed for the performance yet."

"Will there be a performance, Mr. DeVille?" asked Charlie.

Dragonstone froze. He stared at Theopolis. "What does he mean, DeVille?"

Charlie whispered to Theopolis, "If Brack doesn't have a hotel, then you don't have a trick. Joey and I will play his video to the audience that's waiting for you downstairs."

"Think you're clever, don't you, Mr. Hitchcock?" said Theopolis. "Very well. You have won this battle." He turned and walked back to the door of his room. He stopped and shot Charlie a wicked glance. "But the war is not over!" And with a snap of his teeth, he exited the hall.

"Wish I could stay and chat with you youngsters, but I have to be onstage in twenty minutes," said Dragonstone. He hurried down the hall toward the elevators.

"Wow!" said Joey. "That was incredible! What a scoop!"

"You can't show people your video," said Charlie.

"I know that," said Joey. "I need that magician guy to sign a release form first."

"No," said Charlie. "I mean you can't show it ever. Or Brack loses the hotel."

Annie smiled. "Let's go downstairs to watch the show. And then Charlie and I can explain everything that's been going on."

"You got a deal," said Joey.

As they walked back down the hallway, Charlie glanced at the magic carpet design beneath their shoes. A gleaming rectangle of many colors.

He knew the rectangle held the secret to finding his missing friends. He also knew that as soon as he and Annie had convinced Joey Bingham not to show his video, they'd get back on that elevator again.

They had to find the thirteenth floor of the Hocus Pocus Hotel.

ABOUT THE AUTHOR

MICHAEL DAHL grew up reading everything he could find about his hero Harry Houdini, and worked as a magician's assistant when he was a teenager. Even though he cannot disappear, he is very good at escaping things. Dahl has written the popular Library of Doom series, the Dragonblood books, and the Finnegan Zwake series. He currently lives in the Midwest in a haunted house.

ABOUT THE ILLUSTRATOR

LISA K. WEBER is an illustrator currently living in Oakland, California. She graduated from Parsons School of Design in 2000 and then began freelancing. Since then, she has completed many print, animation, and design projects, including graphic novelizations of classic literature, character and background designs for children's cartoons, and textiles for dog clothing.

DISCUSSION QUESTIONS

1. Explain how Charlie knows to look under the stairs for the missing people.

2. Have you seen a magic show? Talk about some of the tricks you saw.

3. Would you stay on the thirteenth floor at the Abracadabra Hotel? Why or why not?

WRITING PROMPTS

1. Try writing about Tyler's disappearance from his point of view. How does the story change? What does Ty see, hear, think, and feel while he is missing?

2. Create your own code to communicate with a friend. What is it? How does it work?

3. Charlie and Annie work together to find the people who disappeared. Write about a time when you worked with someone else to solve a problem.

GLOSSARY

appropriate (uh-PROH-pree-it)—right or suitable

blueprint (BLOO-print)—a model or detailed plan of action

forfeit (FOR-fit)—giving up the right to something

fraud (frawd)—dishonest behavior and tricks that are intended to trick people

illusion (i-LOO-zhuhn)—something that appears to exist but does not; a trick

premiere (pri-MEER)—the first public performance of a show or work of art

puny (PYOO-nee)—small and weak

straitjacket (STREYT-jak-it)—a cover of strong material designed to prevent movement of a person's arms

surveillance (ser-VEYL-uhns)—close watch kept over someone or something

venue (VEN-yoo)—place where an event is held

ZARCON, THE INVISIBLE HERO

The alien hero Zarcon has worked hard to bring criminals to justice. Now it's time for him to go home. With a wave of your magic wand, he disappears and travels back to his own planet.

YOU NEED:
- a colorful handkerchief
- a small action figure
- a secret helper
- a magic wand.

PERFORMANCE:

1. Show Zarcon to the audience and tell them he wants to return to his home planet. Tell them that you're going to help him with a bit of magic. When you're ready for the trick, hold the toy in your hand as shown.

2. Next, place the hanky over your hand to hide Zarcon as shown.

3. Now ask two volunteers to feel under the hanky to make sure Zarcon hasn't disappeared yet.

4. The second person will really be your secret helper. Your helper will secretly take Zarcon from your hand as shown, then hide the toy in his or her pocket. Ask your secret helper, "Is Zarcon still there?" He or she should say, "Yes."

5. After your helper takes Zarcon, wave your magic wand over the hanky. Finally, remove the hanky and show the audience that Zarcon has disappeared!

MAGIC TIP:
Be sure to practice this trick with your helper ahead of time. Make it look smooth and natural and the audience won't suspect a thing.

Like this trick? Learn more in the book *Amazing Magic Tricks: Beginner Level* by Norm Barnhart!